P931f

FRIEND
OR FROG

Marjorie Priceman

Houghton Mifflin Company Boston 1989

Many thanks to
David Macaulay

Library of Congress Cataloging-in-Publication Data

Priceman, Marjorie.
   Friend or frog?

   Summary: When Kate has to find a new home for her
frog, Hilton, her advertisement in the newspaper brings
some alarming responses.
   [1. Frogs—Fiction.   2. Friendship—Fiction]
I. Title.
PZ7.P932Fr   1989   [E]   88-32810
ISBN 0-395-44523-X

Printed in the United States of America

Y 10 9 8 7 6 5 4 3 2 1

Kate's best friend was green and spotted,
which is unusual in a friend but attractive in a frog.
Kate met him on the beach in Florida.
Discovering they had a lot in common,
she invited him north to live with her family.

Being an agreeable sort of frog, he accepted.
He grabbed his one belonging, a towel with the name
HILTON on it. And they were off to New York.

There he made himself at home
in a nicely furnished bowl.
Though he was out of it
more than he was in it,

often showing up in the
most surprising places,
just to lend a hand.

When he wasn't helping out around the house, Hilton often joined Kate for a movie.

They liked dancing after dark, and taking strolls around the block. The neighbors found it strange.

But Hilton and Kate were perfectly happy, until the day Mrs. Elvira Hooper Wiggins came to visit.

"Gracious me! There's a frog in my tea," remarked Mrs. Wiggins.
Then she fainted. Kate's mother was not amused.

Kate woke up shaking. Hilton was not like
other frogs. He had talent and personality.
He would wither away in a swamp.
A suitable home must be found, she decided.
Preferably in the neighborhood.

So Kate placed an ad in the Sunday paper.

Amazing Amphibian For Immediate Adoption:
four inches long, green with brown spots, like new.
Impeccable manners, delightful sense of humor, helpful
around the house. Good starter pet, great gift idea.
Interested parties call 555-8270. Ask for Kate.

But the newspaper charged
fifty cents per word, so
Kate changed the ad to:
FREE FROG 555-8270.

On Sunday morning, three people called.
Kate scheduled the interviews for that
afternoon.

Monsieur Fromage was first to arrive.

"Do you like frogs?" Kate asked.

"More than ice cream," he replied.

So far, so good, thought Kate.

"Have you ever had a frog?"

"Oh, bowls and bowls of them," said Monsieur Fromage.

"I had some today for lunch."

"I beg your pardon," said Kate.

"French-fried frogs' legs. So delicious!" he said.

Kate was alarmed.

"Ha ha," said Monsieur Fromage. "I was only kidding."

But was he?

Next Kate interviewed a boy named Donald.

He peered at Hilton through a magnifying glass.

"Aha!" he exclaimed. "The speckled-back lily leaper!"

"You know a lot about frogs," said Kate.

"Correction," said Donald, "I know *everything* about frogs."

Then he poked. He measured.
He said "Aha!" a lot.
"Well?" said Kate.
"He's perfect," said Donald.
"It's true," said Kate.

"Ideal for my scientific experiments," he said.
"You've made a big mistake," warned Kate.
"I'm a genius," said Donald.
"I never make mistakes.
Besides," he added,
"frogs love science.
Trust me."
But could she?

The three frog lovers grew restless and fidgety.

"I'm not getting any younger," sighed Miss Lavender.

"I have important work to begin," whined Donald.

"It's almost time for my snack," said Monsieur Fromage.

Hilton had heard enough.

There was a splash. And the sound of tiny frog feet.
"Oh dear," cried Kate. "If I don't catch him quick,
   it's the swamp for sure!"

The trail of wet footprints led Kate right after him.
"Hilton, come back here!" she screamed.

Her cry alerted the frog lovers,
and they sprang to their feet.
They chased Hilton in and out of rooms,
up and down stairs, around chairs
and under tables.

They got closer and closer.

"My prince!" screamed Miss Lavender.

"My dinner!" hollered Monsieur Fromage.

"My science project!" squealed Donald.

Hilton was starting to worry.
Then he spotted the box for
Grandma's birthday hat and
hopped inside to hide.

While everyone was looking for Hilton,
Kate's mother came by, tied up the box,
and mailed it off to Florida, first class.

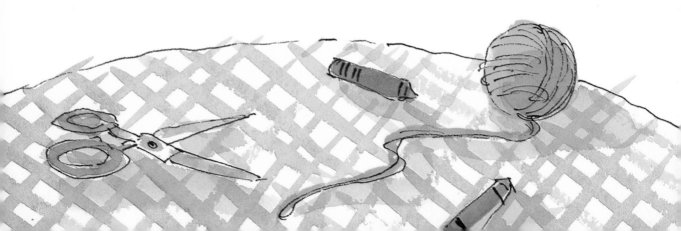

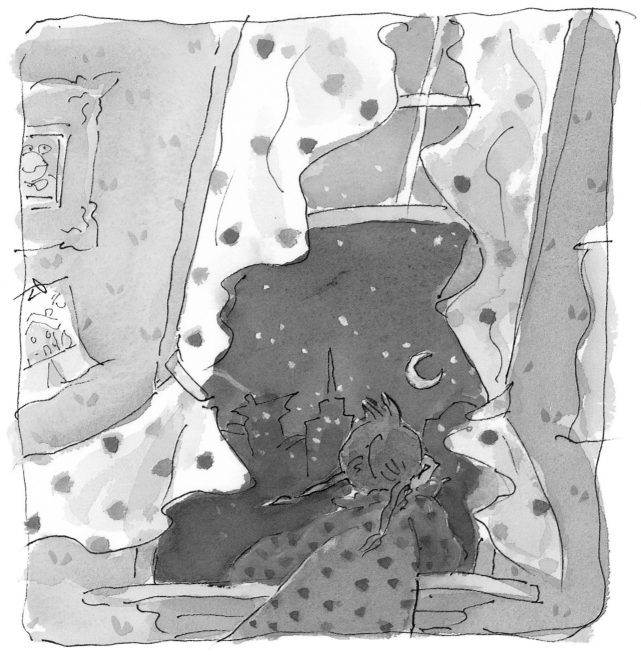

No one could find Hilton, so the frog lovers went home.
Kate missed him terribly. Everything green reminded
her of him. She couldn't look at her string beans
at dinner. She went to her room and stared out the window.

He's out there somewhere, Kate thought. Then she saw
the great frog constellation twinkling brightly in the sky.
As a tear fell from her eye, she realized that you can't really
own a frog, any more than you can own a star. But if you're
lucky enough, maybe you can know one for a little while.

Three days later a postcard
came from Florida. It said:

Dear Kate,
Swamp dwelling surprisingly nice.
Neighbors friendly. Insects delicious.
Wish you were here.
                    H.

And more postcards came each
week, proving that any frog
who's truly a friend will
try to stay in touch.